W9-BUE-101

DISCARDED BY THE LEVI
HEYWOOD MEMORIAL LIBRARY

MaryKate Jordan

LOSING UNCLE TIM

illustrated by Judith Friedman

J
Jord
Parent Shelf

ALBERT WHITMAN & COMPANY, Niles, Illinois

6/90 Brodart 12,95

Text © 1989 by MaryKate Jordan.
Illustrations © 1989 by Judith Friedman.
Published in 1989 by Albert Whitman & Company,
5747 West Howard Street, Niles, Illinois 60648.
Published simultaneously in Canada
by General Publishing, Limited, Toronto.
All rights reserved. Printed in the U.S.A.
Designed by Karen Johnson Campbell.
10 9 8 7 6 5 4 3 2 1

Library of Congress Cataloging-in-Publication Data

Jordan, MaryKate.
Losing Uncle Tim / MaryKate Jordan;
illustrated by Judith Friedman.

p. cm.
Summary: When his beloved Uncle Tim dies of AIDS,
Daniel struggles to find reassurance and understanding
and finds that his favorite grown-up has left him a
legacy of joy and courage.
ISBN 0-8075-4756-5
[1. AIDS (Disease)—Fiction. 2. Death—Fiction.
3. Uncles—Fiction.] I. Friedman, Judith, 1945- ill.
II. Title.
PZ7.J7655Lo 1989   89-5280
[Fic]—dc19   CIP
                                                AC

The text for this book is set in Trump Mediaeval.
The illustrations are in gouache.

For my aunt, Nora, and for my friend, Tim. M.J.
In memory of Eric O'Brian. J.F.

I used to spend a lot of time at my Uncle Tim's antique store. The store was full of neat things Uncle Tim loved. He traveled all over on treasure hunts and brought back toys and clothes and furniture for us to sell.

Uncle Tim was more fun than any other grownup I knew. When I was little, we played outdoors. We played with all the old toys in his store. We sailed wooden ducks on the Housatonic River, and we flew down hills on an old oak sled with red metal runners.

We turned quilts from the store into tents in the woods. It was a long walk from the store to the forest. I was good at stretching my legs to go faster, and Uncle Tim was good at stepping small to go slower.

When I got bigger, we played indoors a lot, at the store and at Uncle Tim's house. I would put Uncle Tim's pennies in an old toy bank. Every time I put a penny in, a little bear would pop out of the top of a tree stump. Uncle Tim always laughed. So did I.

One morning, while I was at the store, some people bought the little bear bank. I felt so bad to see it go that I cried.

"I didn't know you liked that bank so much," Uncle Tim said. "What other toys do you especially care about?"

"The duck with the green head, the sled, and the tent quilts," I said.

"I'll remember, Daniel," Uncle Tim said. "Now, how about a good game of checkers?"

I almost always beat Uncle Tim at checkers. I triple-jumped his last three men that day. "You're a natural checkers champ!" Uncle Tim said.

On cold days, we'd wrap up in quilts and sit in rocking chairs. We'd drink hot cider and rock with our toes pointing toward the fire in the wood stove.

Some days, Uncle Tim laughed and talked a lot. Other days, he didn't have too much to say. Then, one day, he fell asleep right while he was talking. After that, he fell asleep almost every time I saw him. I asked my mom why he was so tired all of a sudden.

Mom didn't say anything for a few seconds. Then she said Uncle Tim's body was getting worn out from a disease called AIDS.

"No!" I yelled back. I'd heard about AIDS, and it sounded pretty bad. "Uncle Tim can't have AIDS! When will he be better?"

Mom put her hand on my shoulder and looked straight into my eyes. "I don't know," she said. "Most people with AIDS don't get better. Most of them eventually die."

"But I don't want Uncle Tim to die," I said.

"Everyone wants him to live," said Mom. "the doctors, his friends, and us. We'll all do our best to take care of him."

Then she held me for a few minutes without saying anything. When I looked up, I could see she was crying.

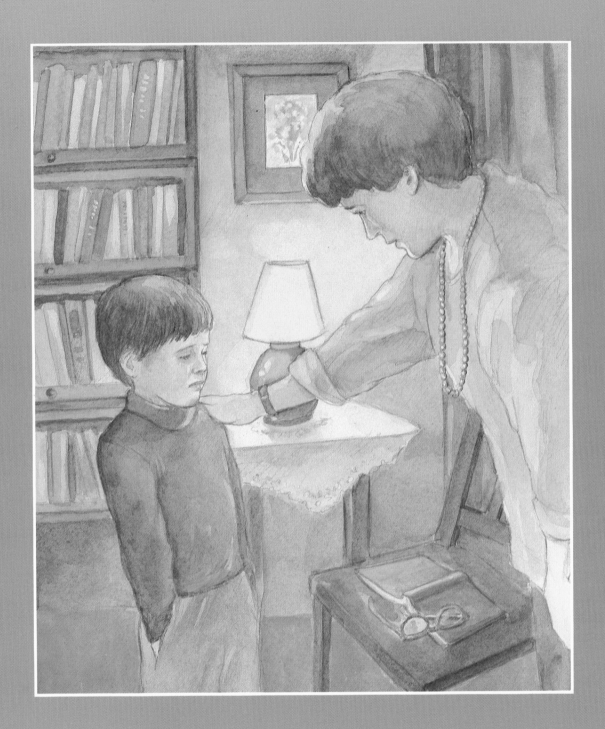

The next time I went to visit Uncle Tim, he looked different to me, somehow, because now I knew he had AIDS. It was the first time I had ever looked at somebody and known he was probably dying.

Uncle Tim asked me to move our rocking chairs over to the window. We watched the sun go down. He told me that when the sun sets in Massachusetts, it's already night in England. And it's already morning in China. "The sun's always shining someplace," Uncle Tim said, "even though we can't always see it."

In the spring, Uncle Tim started to look old, like the toys in his store. There were lots of bottles of pills on the table next to his bed. He was so tired that when he had to go to the bathroom, one of his friends had to help him get up and walk. I got scared and mad. How could something as simple as walking to the bathroom be so hard?

Then I remembered hearing someplace that AIDS was catching. I felt sick to my stomach and sort of prickly all over. Before Uncle Tim got back from the bathroom, I snuck out the door and ran all the way home. I was crying so hard I ran right past Mom and Dad. I dove onto my bed and started hitting the pillow with my fist.

After I hit my pillow for a while, I just lay there on my bed. I pretended that the ceiling was a movie screen, and I could make good movies come out of my eyes. If I really concentrated, I could believe that Uncle Tim was okay. I was pretending so hard I nearly jumped out of my skin when Dad knocked on my door.

"Can I come in?" he asked.

"If you want to," I said.

Dad sat down on the edge of my bed. "Did you see Uncle Tim today?" he asked.

"Yup," I replied, staring at a spot of mud on the tip of my left sneaker. "But maybe I won't go again for a while."

Dad didn't say anything.

"Uncle Tim can't even walk to the bathroom," I went on. "And maybe I'm going to get AIDS from being over there so much." I looked up at my dad. "Am I? Am I going to catch AIDS from Uncle Tim?"

Dad shook his head.

I was still afraid. "I go to Uncle Tim's a lot," I argued. "I hug him. Sometimes we have dinner together."

Dad put both arms around me and held me tight. "It's safe for you to be with Tim," he said. "You can sit close to him and hug him. You can have dinner with him. Mom and I asked Tim's doctor how safe it is for us to be close to him. The doctor said you can't catch AIDS just by taking care of someone."

"I'm glad," I said. "I really want to see Uncle Tim."

"He really wants to see you, too," Dad said.

"Want to play checkers?" I asked Uncle Tim the next day. He nodded and sat up. I set up the board on the table next to his bed. We played for about five minutes. "You're trying to let me win," Uncle Tim said.

I chewed on my lower lip. "I thought maybe if I didn't win so much you might not die."

Uncle Tim looked into my eyes like Mom did when she told me he had AIDS. "Maybe I'll die and maybe I won't," Uncle Tim said. "But you don't throw the game. That's the only sure way to lose. Understand?"

I played the best I could.

"Yahoo!" Uncle Tim hollered when he won.

"Did you let me win all those other times?" I asked, suddenly scared it might be true.

"Nope," he answered. "You're a natural, but this game was mine."

I put the checkers set and the board back into the box. "Take that checkers set home with you," Uncle Tim said. "You can teach somebody else how to play."

I was glad Uncle Tim gave me his checkers set but sad we wouldn't play anymore. "Thanks, Uncle Tim. I love you," I said.

"I love you, too, Daniel," he answered.

The next three times I came to visit, Uncle Tim was always asleep. I said hi anyway and told him what was going on. The last time, a friend of his walked in and heard me. I felt stupid but it turned out okay. He said people who are in a coma, the special kind of sleep Uncle Tim was in, can often hear even though they can't answer. That made me feel good, not stupid.

"Goodbye, Uncle Tim," I said out loud. "I'm going home now."

My Uncle Tim died the next day.

I went to his funeral. Everybody in the family was there. "How will Uncle Tim eat breakfast in that box?" my little cousin Jeremy asked.

"He doesn't have to eat anymore," I said.

All the grownups talked in big whispers. Grandma and Grandpa cried. So did my mom. So did my dad. So did I.

"I wish dying was like sunset," I said to Mom as we left the funeral home. "I wish Uncle Tim would come back again in the morning."

"I wish he could, Daniel," Mom said. We sat real close together all during the drive to the cemetery.

Before my Uncle Tim's body was buried, the minister said some prayers. Then she added, "The hardest part of having Tim die is not having his body here to hug." She said that the part of him that's really Uncle Tim is still alive, but not like we were used to when we could see him.

Maybe Uncle Tim is like the sun, just shining somewhere else.

The grownups read a paper called Uncle Tim's will. It told us what he wanted done with his store and his things. It said Uncle Tim had given me the green-headed duck, the sled, and one of the tent quilts. He remembered, just like he said he would.

My mom and dad brought everything home. I put the sled down in the basement. It can stay there till the snow comes.

The quilt is right here on my bed. The duck sits on my desk, next to the checkers set.

My desk is in front of a window. Sometimes I sit there early in the morning and think about Uncle Tim. "The sun's always shining someplace," he used to say. I can almost hear him tell me, "When the sun comes up in Massachusetts, it's already morning in England. And it's already evening in China."

I miss him.

Maybe when I grow up, I'll go to England and to China. Maybe I'll teach little kids how to play checkers. Maybe I'll teach Jeremy.

Maybe I'll own a store. Or I might do something else. I don't know what yet. But I'll do something I love. Just like Uncle Tim.

ABOUT THE AUTHOR

MaryKate Jordan lives in the Berkshire hills of western Massachusetts where she is a minister. When she was eight years old, she decided she wanted to write stories for children when she grew up. The death of a favorite hospice client and the death of a well-loved aunt, just five months apart, were the catalysts for writing *Losing Uncle Tim*.

ABOUT THE ARTIST

Judith Friedman has illustrated many magazines and textbooks, but her real love is illustrating books for children. She also teaches children's book illustration to students at the School of the Art Institute of Chicago. *Losing Uncle Tim* is her seventh book for Albert Whitman.